# IN THE SHADOWS OF
# MOUNTAINS

# IN THE SHADOWS OF
# M O U N T A I N S

\*   \*   \*

*Ahtna Stories from the Copper River*

Collected & Edited By

## John E. Smelcer

Foreword By

## Gary Snyder

*Fred Ewan*

The Ahtna Heritage Foundation

# IN THE SHADOWS OF MOUNTAINS

© 1997 by John E. Smelcer

Library of Congress Cataloging-in-Publication Data:

Smelcer, John E., 1963-
*In the Shadows of Mountains*
*Ahtna Stories from the Copper River*
1. Alaska Native Myths— Ahtna. 2. Oral History— Ahtna.
3. Folklore. 4. Am. Indian— Athabaskan. 5. Alaska
I. Title

ISBN  0-9656310-0-1

*The Ahtna Heritage Foundation*
*P. O. Box 213*
*Glennallen, AK 99588*

Printed in the United States of America

# Contents

*Dedicated to the Ahtna People
in every village, everywhere, whether
they dwell in the shadows of these
mountains, or others.*

# Foreword

Tucked back between the Chugach and the St. Elias Mountains, with the Wrangells to the east; up in the valleys and tributaries of the Copper River, and hidden south of the main route over to the Yukon drainage, is Ahtna Country. As editor John Smelcer says, perhaps the last Native group in North America to be contacted by the Euro-Americans, so remote they were. A self-sufficient and self-governing People tucked into a far corner of glaciers, mountains, and spruce woods; little seen, little known. A country that ranges from the edge of the sub-boreal taiga through peaks and canyons to the enormous icefields of the monster coastal ranges facing the Gulf of Alaska.

This neat, compact book brings us their myths and tales. As is usually true in the world of traditional story, they are both unique to place, and also cosmopolitan. They belong to the broader realm of the Athabaskan language family that stretches from the Yukon basin to the mountains of southern Arizona, with a pocket even in coastal California. So, many of the stories are variants widely-told tales; some even belong to the archaic international world of stories that reaches from Virginia to Finland, and down into Africa.

These little family-told narratives introduce us again to "Way long ago," a place that will be familiar forever— where baby Raven plays on the dirt floor (like baby Krishna) biding his time to steal the sun, stars, and moon that are bound in the fancy boxes of his grandfather. Where the web of magic and relationship is such that Fox's daughter can be married to Raven, where kindness to a little mouse will be repaid tenfold richly in bundles of food; where the tricks can be fierce as when fox fools the wolves into eating their greedy sister. "You ate your sister!" he taunts. This primary world of the self-governing Peoples of North America is not for sissies. The lessons are hard, but true.

Raven is the creator. He "created salmon to join the streams and rivers to the sea" — so ingenious and far-thinking he was. But his lessons are often a matter of teaching by bad, rather than good example. The world of these tales is totally moral, but via a hard-core realism that rings honest to our actual situation— where Creation is possibly partly mischief, and we must deal with a world of complexities. But even Raven's mistakes can sometimes be poignant, as when he falls in love with a beautiful goose maiden, and try as he may, cannot keep up with her when it's time to fly south.

The Ahtna People give us again this gift of an ancient, totally present, real world where we walk with archetypal fox, rabbit, porcupine, wolf, camprobber, bear . . . through the Imagination we human beings (and maybe all the other critters too!) all share.

Gary Snyder,
UC Davis, February, 1997

2

In this map can be seen the various indigenous language groups of Alaska. Eleven groups, all in the interior, are the Athabaskan Indian languages of which Ahtna is one. Only the Dena'ina' (sometimes spelled "Tanaina") region borders the ocean.

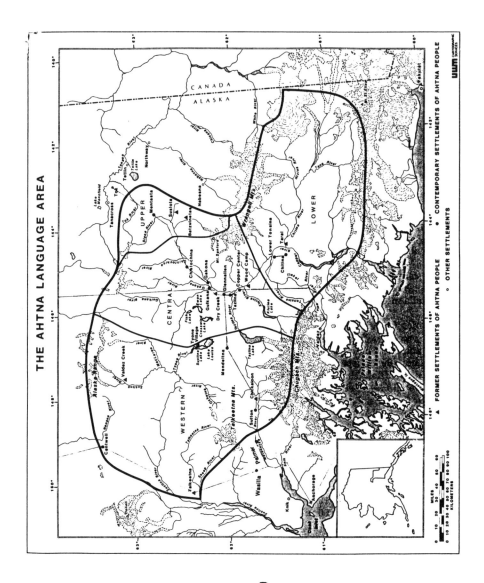

# THE AHTNA LANGUAGE AREA

▲ FORMER SETTLEMENTS OF AHTNA PEOPLE    ● CONTEMPORARY SETTLEMENTS OF AHTNA PEOPLE

○ OTHER SETTLEMENTS

# Introduction

Our stories tell much about us. They teach us who we are. They define our place in the natural world, and they establish a history, an origin for many of our beliefs, traditions, and customs. Indeed, in attempting to understand who we are, every human culture has a corpus of myth to define existence. The two dozen retellings in this book represent the most complete collection of our stories ever assembled. They come from the Ahtna people themselves— from interviews, historical records and notes, and from previously printed material.

While many Native tribes in the continental states no longer live on traditionally-ancestral lands because they were displaced by the American government in previous centuries, no Alaska Native Peoples have been so removed. For the most part, our tribes and villages are in the same geographic region as they have existed for hundreds, even thousands of years. We are a people tied to our land. In many ways this union defines our very lives— the way we view the land, subsist from it, and how we teach our children these values.

The Ahtna People were perhaps the last Indian tribe discovered in North America. As an inland Athabaskan culture, we lived in a country untouched and unimpacted from outside non-Native influences until 1885 when Lt. Henry Allen first made his way, torturously at times, into the heart of our country. The first wave of outsiders didn't really occur

5

until the mid-to-late 1890's. In some ways, the things that have so negatively affected other American Indian tribes in the United States are only in the past fifty years or less beginning to irrevocably affect ours.

Archaeologists say that Ahtna have lived in this region, in *Atna' Nen'*— Ahtna country— for several thousand years. In that time we named every place in the country; every stream, creek, river, and lake. Every mountain, hill, and bluff has a name that our ancestors gave to it. Two predominant landmarks denote our country: the Wrangell St. Elias Mountain Range and the Copper River. Our very name comes from the latter. They dominate our landscape.

For many countless generations we have lived along the edge of the Copper River and its tributaries, and we have lived and died in the shadows of those mountains— mountains which have borne Indian names throughout the memory of a People. We called them *K'eɬt'aeni, Hwniidi K'eɬt'aeni,* and *Hwdaandi Keɬt'aeni.* After contact, however, our names were lost to new names given to our country, names given by newcomers with no history on the land. Sanford Nicolai best summed it up when he said at a potlatch in December, 1977:

> . . . all this time thousands of years, Indians look up and think that it is Khultane *(K'eɬt'aeni)*— for hundreds of generations our forefathers look up and think Mount Kulthane; but Indians not very smart. First white man come along, he look up and say, Ah, Hah, Mount Sanford . . . and Mount Sanford it is today, my people.

Times are changing rapidly and negatively. We are losing our heritage with every television set and radio that is turned on. Every commercial we watch or hear tells us that we should become something else. And everything we watch, read, or hear is in English. Our language has fewer than ninety speakers, and there is little interest by our youth and young adults to revive it.

*The author discusses Ahtna pronunciation with Fred Ewan at Camp*

We recognize these losses. We are surrounded by them. While some efforts have been made to rekindle our ways, perhaps none better do so than this collection. Our traditional stories, like those of any culture, do much more than simply relate mytho-historic events or tell fascinating acts of heroism and creation. These same narratives were told to youth to teach them— a kind of cultural primer. While the stories themselves had meaning and significance, so too did the actual telling itself; for it was from storytelling by family members where young listeners became captivated enough to learn the lesson, while at the same time, and perhaps more importantly, they also learned the language.

This collection uses Ahtna words (mostly central dialect) throughout its pages so that its readers, Ahtna or not, might briefly be introduced to our faltering language and its beauty and intricacies; and in doing so, stave off extinction a while longer; because, as linguist Ken Hale put it, "The loss of a language is part of the more general loss being suffered by the world, the loss of diversity of all things."

# Acknowledgements

This collection is not the product of a single individual's work. These are the stories of a People — passed down for generations so that our children may know the natural world around them and at the same time learn to keep our Indian heritage alive by passing them on to future generations. It is a sad fact that most of our tribal members born after the middle of this century don't even know these stories. But traditions have a way of being revived in the face of renewed interest when eminent loss becomes all too clear.

Although the author ultimately assembled and edited this volume, individual stories and variations were retold by members of the Ahtna Tribe from villages in the Copper River region, and some are borrowed from *Atna' Yanida'a* (1979) and *Indian Stories* (1982), both of which are out-of-print (we are reprinting *Indian Stories* this year). It is important to note that stories such as these are often considered property of specific clans; and as such, are to be retold only by members of specific clans. This is true within Ahtna society as it is among other Alaska Native tribes. But there is a danger in restricting storytelling among clans. My father's clan is *Taltsiine* (Talcheena: "Comes from the sea"). Sadly, there are very few remaining *Taltsiine* Clan members left. Should those stories considered property of *Taltsiine* be allowed to disappear forever when the last clan member retells a myth for the very last time? Should the stories of any People suffer such a fate?

A collection such as this may well outlast those who told them to become— perhaps— the only lasting record of our storytelling tradition.

Because these stories are often told by different members within a clan, or even within the tribe, and because they are told at different times, places, and occasions, there are often differences in the retellings. These variations are part of the tradition. Indeed, as tribal members mature, certain parts of a story may become more significant to them and, therefore, they focus more upon that significance than one might otherwise. I say this because at Joe Goodlataw's (Chief Goodlataw's brother) potlatch, I was reminded that some of these versions differ from what someone from another village or clan might have heard when they were growing up.

This project was funded and supported by Ahtna, Inc., our federally-recognized Native corporation, by the Ahtna Heritage Foundation Board of Directors, and by a distinguished committee of Ahtna elders who recommended regional elders for consultation and for personal interviews during this project, as well as for other important language projects.

Profit from the sale of this book shall be given to a scholarship fund for Ahtna-descended students to attend college, and shall also help support future heritage projects such as Culture Camp.

This collection could not have been made possible without the support of the following organizations and individuals:

Ahtna, Inc.                          John Billum
Ahtna Heritage Foundation            Molly Billum
Roy Ewan                             Mary Smelcer-Wood

Nicholas Jackson
Veronica Nicholas
Carolyn Craig
Donald Johns
Eileen Ewan
Cecilia Larson
Susan Larson
Lucille Brenwick
Ben Neeley
Herbert Smelcer
Louise Tansy Mayo
Jake Tansy

Morrie Secondchief
Fred Ewan
Fred Sinyon
Millie Buck
Markle Pete
Harry Johns
Ruth Johns
Larry Vienneau
Dale Seeds
James Kari
Gary Snyder
Barre Toelken

An Ahtna woman dips for salmon in the dangerously swift waters of the Copper River. Photo circa 1910.

# AHTNA STORIES FROM THE
# COPPER RIVER

# How Raven Killed the Whale

*Although Ahtna's traditional territory does not border the ocean, this story is still part of our narrative literature (it also appears in the oral history of several other southeast Alaska Native Peoples). Interestingly, my family's clan is* Taltsiine (Talcheena), "*Came from the sea.*" *Perhaps this story, like others, first came to Ahtna country via migrations of families and clans from other regions. This version was told by* Fred Sinyon *to a group of youth at Culture Camp while sitting around the campfire one evening.*

As usual, *Saghani Ggaay*, Trickster Raven, was hungry. He had heard of a large whale near an island and so he went to see it for himself. The people in the nearby village were afraid of it. They were so afraid that they would not take their boats out to fish.

Raven flew to the place and carefully watched the whale, all the time thinking how he could trick it so that he could eat it. That smart bird knew that he would have lots to eat if he could kill the whale. Finally, an idea came to him. He flew into the forest and gathered dry wood which he tied to a pack on his back. Then Raven flew out across the water to a rock near the whale.

"Come closer, Cousin Whale, so that I may speak with you," requested the sly black bird.

15

*Tełaani* heard the sound and opened his eyes. He had been resting in the sunshine. When he saw the small bird who was speaking to him, Whale swam closer to the rock to speak. You, see, animals could speak to each other back then.

"What do you want?" asked the whale whose rest was interupted by the bird.

"I have come to tell you that we are cousins," Raven said.

"That is impossible. You are a puny bird and I am a whale. We are not cousins," replied Whale.

"It is true. We are cousins," said Raven. "I can prove it."

*Tełaani* was curious, so he asked *Saghani Ggaay* to prove their relation.

"If you will open your mouth," said Raven, "you will see how our throats are the same shape, which proves that we are cousins."

As Raven spoke, he opened his mouth to let the whale see his tiny throat.

Although the giant Killer Whale did not believe that they had anything in common, he slowly opened his mouth with its many teeth. When his mouth was opened just far enough, Raven quickly ran into his mouth and down his long throat. He was still wearing his bundle of dry wood which he now used to build him a small

*Fred Sinyon tells stories at Camp*

fire. He cut slices of meat from inside the whale and began to cook it over the fire.

16

Whale knew that he had been tricked. He begged Raven not to eat his heart, this way he would stay alive. Raven agreed and spent many days inside the whale eating whenever he was hungry, which was most of the time.

After most of the meat was cooked and eaten, Raven began to think about getting out of the whale. One day, Whale told Raven that they where in shallow water and near land. Raven saw this as his chance to get out. He took his knife and cut out the whale's heart, and the poor whale died. After a short time the waves pushed Telaani's great body onto a pebble beach. Raven cut a hole in the side of the whale just big enough to squeeze through and then he walked into the sunshine and flew high into the air, looking around for something else to eat.

*Saghani Ggaay* (sa-gaw-nee guy) "Little Trickster Raven"
*Telaani* (te-klaw-nee) "Whale"

# Raven Steals the Stars, Moon, and Sun

*Just as western religion suggests that the world was void of light in the very beginning, so too was the Ahtna world before Raven stole the sun, the moon, and the stars and released them. There are ethnographic accounts of this narrative in almost all Alaska Native mythologies. In some versions Raven turns himself into a hemlock needle to impregnate the young woman, while in others he becomes a spruce needle, a small fish, and even a piece of fine moss. Recorded as early as 1850 in Sitka by Heinrich J. Holmberg, this version was told to me by my 80 year old, full-blood Ahtna grandmother,* Mary Smelcer-Wood, *daughter of* Tazlina Joe.

My mother told me this story about Raven. Not the black bird we see today. This Raven was like a god. He was the most powerful of all beings. He had made the animals, fish, trees, even the mountains and waters. He had made all living creatures, but they were all living in darkness because he had not made *na'aay*, the sun.

One day Raven learned that there was a great chief living along the banks of a distant river who had the sun, the moon, and the stars in three carved boxes. The great chief also had a very beautiful daughter. Both the princess and the treasures were well guarded.

This Raven, *Saghani Ggaay*, knew that he must trick the chief in order to steal his treasure, so he decided to turn himself into a grandchild of the great chief. He flew upon a tall tree near their house and waited. When the princess came to a small pond to get water, Raven turned himself into a small speck. Thus disguised, he fell into the girl's drinking cup. When she drank the water, she also drank the speck which was really Raven. Inside the chief's daughter, Raven became a baby and soon the young woman bore a son who was so dearly loved by the chief that he gave him whatever he asked for. But because the princess had no husband, the family had to hide the baby. And what a different baby it was. In no time at all it was grown and could speak.

The stars, the moon, and the sun were held in three very beautiful and ornately carved wooden boxes which sat on the dirt floor of the house. The one grandchild who was actually the Raven, wanted to play with the stars and the moon and wouldn't stop his crying until that grandfather

*My grandmother tells me stories*

gave them to him. As soon as he had them, though, Raven threw them up through the smoke-hole. Instantly, they scattered across the sky. Although the grandfather was unhappy, he loved his grandson too much to punish him for what he had done.

Now that he had tossed the stars and the moon out the smokehole, the little grandson began crying for the box containing the sun. He cried and cried and would not stop. He was actually making himself sick because he was crying so much. Finally, the grandfather gave him the box and Raven played with it for a long time. Suddenly, though, he turned

20

himself back into a bird and flew up through the smoke-hole with the box.

Once he was far away from the small village, Raven heard people speaking in the darkness and approached them.

"Who are you and would you like to have light?" he asked those people who lived in the dark.

They said that he was a liar; that no one could give light.

To show them that he was telling the truth, Raven opened the ornately carved box and let sunlight into the world. The people were so frightened by it that they fled to every corner of the world. This is why there are Raven's people everywhere.

Now there are stars, the moon, and the sun and it is no longer dark all of the time.

*na'aay* (naw-eye) "sun, moon" [used in the naming of months]
*Saghani Ggaay* (sa-gaw-nee guy) "Little Trickster Raven"

# Raven and Loon: The Necklace Story

*This particular version of a popular* Ahtna *myth is one of my favorites as it was told to me in* Mendeltna *by my grandmothers,* Mary Smelcer-Wood and Morrie Secondchief. *There was a magical quality to the telling as both women recalled the story from their youth and took turns telling segments and seeking affirmation from the other. Versions of this narrative can be found in the mythologies of other North American Indian groups, including* Eyak, *which is a neighbor of* Ahtna. Ruth Johns *of* Copper Center *later told me a slightly different version.*

In the time very long ago, when animals could speak and people had not yet been created, Raven and Loon were good friends and visited with one another often. Back in those days both birds were white. They were white all over.

One day Raven was flying around looking for food when he saw Loon—*Dadzeni*—swimming on a lake. He landed and asked his friend to come and visit him. The other bird swam to shore to talk with his friend.

"Let's paint each other," said the white Raven.

They looked around and found some black mud along the lake's edge, and with it Raven began to paint the white Loon's back and feathers black with white speckles, and then he made a pretty necklace around Loon's neck, his *uk'os*.

"You look so wonderful!" exclaimed Raven when finished.

23

*Dadzeni* looked at himself in the smooth lake's reflection and saw how pretty he was and that he had a beautiful necklace. But his head and chest was still white.

Raven asked his friend, "Please, paint me just as I have painted you so that I will look as pretty."

Loon took some mud and began painting. But Loon wasn't as good as Raven and he could not make him as pretty. Even though he tried very hard, he could not paint as well as his friend.

When he was done Raven looked at himself in the water and saw that he was all black. Every part of him was black; even his feet, head, and beak was black. He did not even have a necklace around his neck.

*My great Aunt Morrie at Tazlina*

He began to jump up and down yelling at Loon.

"Look at me! Look at me!" he screamed. "I am all black. You did not paint me like I painted you. I do not even have a pretty necklace!"

The angry Raven chased Loon all over trying to get him. He chased that Loon around that lake all day long. All that time the loon was saying that he was sorry.

Finally, Loon flew out to the middle of the lake where his angry friend could not get him. You see, Ravens can't swim. Raven stood on the beach and shouted at him. Then he picked up a handful of mud and threw it very far and hit Loon right on the head! He got him on the head. When he was tired of yelling,

Raven flew away and they have not been friends again.

Since that time, Raven has been black all over and Loon has a black head and a pretty necklace.

*Dadzeni* (dad-zee-nee) "Loon"
*uk'os* (oo-kos) "neck"

*Ruth Johns of Copper Center tells stories*

# The Mouse Story

*I have encountered similar retellings of this story in neighboring Athabaskan tribe's oral traditions; especially in Dena'ina (sometimes spelled "Tanaina"). This was told to me years ago by the late Walter Charley, after whom we named our Ahtna Foundation Scholarship.*

Long ago, in a small village, there lived a young man. The people of the village worked very hard all summer putting away food for the long winter. They caught salmon with long dip nets, and they used fishtraps to catch other fish, too. They worked like this preparing for winter.

One day this man was walking around looking for berries. In the brush beside him he saw a small mouse—*dluuni*—carrying a large fish egg—*k'uun'*—in its mouth. The mouse was struggling very hard to cross a log in its path.

The man saw this and helped the mouse. He gently lifted it over the log and placed it on the other side. The mouse quickly ran into the brush and was gone.

Winter came too early that year. It was cold and there wasn't enough food put away. Half way through winter the food began to run out and the people became weak and sick. Surely they would not survive the winter.

One day, while the young man was out looking for anything to eat, he came upon a small house. Smoke was coming from its smokehole. It was a very small house.

The young man heard a voice coming from inside which told him to turn around three times with his eyes closed. The man did this and became small enough to go through the tiny door — *hwdatnetaani*. Inside, stood a man in a brown fur coat.

"We were expecting you. Come in. Sit down," he said.

The young man sat down and listened.

"Your people have no food. It is a very hard winter for them. But I will help you," said the strange man.

The man brought out a small pack which he began to fill with berries and fish meat and grease. He gave it to the young Indian man from the village who asked why he was doing this.

"This summer you helped me. When I was carrying home a large fish egg for my family, you helped me across a fallen tree. Because you helped me then, I am helping you now."

The young man remembered helping a little *dlunni* and understood that this was that same mouse. He went outside and became big again, but the pack was still small.

"I thank you for this gift, but it is not enough to feed even me." That is what the Indian said.

The Mouse Man replied, "When you return to your village, leave the pack outside for the night and sing this song which I will teach you. In the morning it will become a large pile of food."

The young man did this and he saved his village from starvation because he had helped a small animal.

*dluuni* (dloo-nee) "mouse"
*k'uun'* (k-oon) "fish egg" [pronounced as two syllables]
*hwdatnetaani* (dot-net-taw-nee) "door"

# When Raven Was Killed

*My grandmother,* Mary Smelcer-Wood, *told me this unique story several years ago. I have not encountered a similar version of this particular narrative anywhere, which does not imply that other versions don't exist—only that I have not found them.*

Long ago, way back in the time when animals spoke, there was this Raven. This wasn't the same raven you see flying around nowadays. He was magical, powerful—both creator and destroyer. We call him *Saghani Ggaay,* "Little Trickster Raven."

Well, *Saghani Ggaay* had played so many tricks on mankind for so long that one day a chief—*kaskae*—decided to kill him. The chief invited Raven to visit him at his village. When the black bird wasn't paying attention, the chief threw a skin bag over Raven and tied it tightly shut so that the troublesome bird could not escape.

With the heavy pack on his back, the man began to climb a very steep and high mountain. We say *dghelaay* in Ahtna. It was very dark inside the bag and Raven could not see. He asked the man what he was doing, but the chief ignored him.

As the man climbed higher, Raven spoke out again.

"Where are you taking me?" he asked.

The chief just kept on climbing.

"I can tell that you are climbing a high mountain," insisted

Raven. "Why are you carrying me there? What are you going to do to me?" Raven was worried.

The man ignored him still and continued to climb.

Raven warned the chief that he would be sorry if he killed him, saying that bad things would befall his clan.

When the chief was on top of the mountain, he threw the skin bag with Raven inside over the steep side. As it fell, it struck the cliff and ripped open. Raven was torn to pieces by the jagged rocks as he crashed to the ground below. The chief had killed Raven!

When the chief returned to his village, he showed his people the pieces of *Saghani Ggaay* so that they would know what he had done. All of the villagers called him a great chief for killing the mischievous trickster. For several days the village celebrated.

Finally, though, some people began to notice that all of the water was gone. They went to the river, but it was dry. They went to a lake, and it too was empty. There was no water to be found anywhere!

The people began to become thirsty. They knew that they could not live long without water. One day, they asked a shaman why the water had vanished. The shaman told them that it was because the chief had killed Raven. Now the villagers were not happy that Raven was dead. They wanted him back before everyone died.

The shaman told the chief that he had to put Raven's pieces back together again. When he had done this, Raven jumped instantly to life again! He hopped up and down and started to fly away. But then he stopped and asked the chief why he had been brought back to life.

"All of the water has gone," he replied. "Only you can return it."

Raven flew up into the air, higher and higher, and then he spoke down to the man.

"Look around you, there is water everywhere."

The villagers turned towards the river and lake and saw that they were filled with water again.

As Raven flew into the distance, the chief yelled to him, "We will never try to kill you again!"

To this day, because of that promise, Indians do not hunt or kill ravens.

*Saghani Ggaay* (sa-gaw-nee guy)  "Trickster Raven in *yanida'a* stories"
*kaskae* (kask-a)  "chief, wealthy man"  [a pronounced as in 'cat']
*dgheluuy* (ga-lie)  "mountain"

# How Porcupine Got Quills

*Similar versions of this origin myth occur in many of the eleven Athabaskan tribes of Alaska. Indeed, in the oral histories of almost all indigenous peoples of the world there are origin myths explaining how things, especially animals, came to be.*

When porcupine was first created by Raven, he had soft hair. He didn't have the sharp quills he now has.

Because *Nuuni* had no means to protect himself, he was always being teased by other animals, especially by Bear and Wolf who bothered him the most. They would take his food away and leave him hungry, or they would harass him just for the fun of it.

It happened that way for a long time until poor Porcupine learned a few ways to escape from *Tsaani's* and *Tikaani's* tauntings. His best trick was to climb a tree where neither Bear nor Wolf could reach him. But sometimes there was not a tall enough or strong enough tree nearby, so *Tsaani* and *Tikaani* would steal his food again. Also, *Nuuni* was too slow to run away from his enemies. He was really having a rough time of it!

One summer day, while Bear and Wolf were teasing him, they shoved him into a hole full of mud. When Porcupine came out of the hole his soft hair was covered with mud. *Tsaani* and *Tikaani* laughed at him and ran away with his food again.

Since there was no river nearby and because it was such a hot summer day, *Nuuni's* hair soon dried— becoming very stiff and brittle.

The next day Bear saw Porcupine walking down a trail. When he came over to push him down as he always did, he was quite surprised when his paws touched Porcupine's hair. Bear roared in pain and ran away.

From that time on, Bear and Wolf never bothered *Nuuni* again, and all porcupines have sharp quills— *q'ok*— so that bigger animals cannot hurt them or take away their food as they so easily used to do.


*Nuuni*   (new-nee)   "Porcupine"
*Tsaani*   (chaw-nee)   "Grizzly Bear"
*Tikaani*   (tik-a-nee)   "Wolf"
*q'ok*   (kee*awk)   "quills"   [*pronounced as one syllable]

# The Blind Man and the Loon

*The story of* The Blind Man and the Loon *is perhaps one of the most common of Alaska Native myths, second only to* Raven Steals the Sun, Stars, and the Moon. *Accounts of this story appear in* Yupik, Inupiaq, Upper Tanana, Tanaina, Eyak, *and* Ahtna *ethnography. Because* Eyak *is a neighboring tribe, and because* Ahtna *historically traded with them, it is no wonder that their versions are so similar. Like many narratives, it teaches a moral lesson: "Don't be greedy and be kind to those less fortunate."*

A husband and wife once lived inland along the Copper River. The husband was blind, and so the wife had to work hard to gather enough food for them. Because the man was blind, the two had not had any game meat for a long time. One day, though, the wife saw a large moose walking by.

"*Deniigi* is walking by," she whispered.

"Quick," said the husband, "hand me my bow and arrows."

The wife gave them to him. Because she was not strong enough to draw back the bowstring, she had to let the husband shoot. But because he could not see, the wife had to guide his aim.

"Is that good?" he asked her. "Am I aiming at the moose?"

"Yes," she replied. "You are aiming correctly."

The blind man let loose the arrow and instantly he heard the unmistakable sound of the arrow striking the animal's side. The heavy moose lurched forward and then fell down dead.

The wife did not tell her husband the truth. Instead, she had a plan.

"Quick, husband," she said, "it is running away. Shoot again."

The wife helped him aim again. But this time the arrow hit the ground because there was no moose where she had pointed him. She lied to him saying how poorly he had shot.

"You missed it! It got away," she said insultingly.

She told him to stand where he was while she gathered the two arrows. The wife pulled the bloody arrow from the moose's side and wiped it clean in the grass. Then she stuck it in the mud along the riverbank and took it back to her blind husband.

He smelled the tip. "It smells like blood," he told her.

"No," she replied. "You only hit the mud. You did not kill the moose."

She took her husband back to their camp near a small lake behind the river. Then she went back to cut off pieces of the moose for herself. She was not going to tell him the truth. She was going to eat all of the meat and not share any with him.

This went on for days, her eating the meat by herself, until one day the blind man heard a voice coming from the lake.

"Come here," it said.

This startled the man because he did not know anyone was there.

He stood and answered the voice, "I am blind, I cannot see."

The voice replied, " Come here. You can feel your way."

The man cautiously found his way to the lake's edge. It was a giant loon who spoke to him. It spoke again.

"Sit down on my back and hold on to my neck feathers."

The blind man did as he said and *Dadzeni* dove under the water with him and swam around the lake twice. When he came up for air, the loon spoke to him.

"Now, look around," it said.

The man opened his eyes.

"I can see a little," he said excitedly.

"Close your eyes again and hold your breath," demanded the loon.

The two dove under water again and swam around the lake once more. This time when the loon came up the blind man could see perfectly! He thanked the magical bird, promised never to hunt his relatives, and walked back to find his wife to tell her the good news. When he found her he saw that she was boiling some meat and he saw the dead moose that he had killed in the bushes nearby. She had lied to him and now she was not even going to share the food with him. This made him very angry.

When the wife saw him she nervously said, "I was just cooking some meat for you."

The husband was so mad because she had tricked him that he shoved her head into the boiling pot and killed her.

From then on he always had good luck and was a great hunter.

*Deniigi* (den-nig-ee) "Moose"
*Dadzeni* (dad-zee-nee) "Loon"

# Fox and the Greedy Wolverine

*This story, first recorded by John Billum in Atna' Yanida'a, is very similar to one told in Tlingit oral history. In the Tlingit version, though, the characters are human, and a greedy young daughter-in-law turns into an owl as her punishment. Fox's name in this story, Ciił Hwyaa, is not the literal translation for the animal. Instead, it is a nickname for this mythic character often used in Ahtna storytelling.*

A very long time ago, in *yanida'a*, Fox was married and had several children. They all lived in the woods where they hunted for food. But things had not been good for *Ciił Hwyaa* lately. Fox had not brought any meat home in a while even though he hunted all of the time.

During this hungry time, Wolverine— *Nałtsiis*—came to visit. He asked Fox if he could marry one of his daughters. Fox and his wife thought about this and they agreed to give her to him. Because they didn't have enough meat, they gave her away thinking that at least Wolverine would feed her.

One day Wolverine went out hunting. After a time he returned to the village with two beavers. Everyone was happy. Now they would all eat well. Wolverine skinned the beavers and began to cook the meat. His new mother-in-law came and asked for a piece of meat. She thought surely her new son-in-law would share with his new family. But that greedy *Nałtsiis* did not intend to share any of his meat. Instead, he threw a piece of old, dried up moose leg bone at her.

"Here. Cook that!" he said to his wife's mother.

The mother-in-law ran home to tell her husband what had happened. Fox agreed that she had been treated badly, but told her that she should ask again tomorrow.

The next day Wolverine again insulted his mother-in-law.

And the day after that he did the same thing. That greedy Wolverine didn't share any of his meat— not even with his wife. Fox and his wife were very angry. They had given their daughter to Wolverine thinking that he would at least provide for her and act properly towards his in-laws.

The following evening Fox went hunting and he saw moose tracks. He followed the tracks in the fresh snow until he saw that Wolverine was hunting *Deniigi*, too. From a hill he watched as *Naltsiis* chased the moose and then quickly grew tired and let it escape.

On his way back to the village he passed Fox and told him how he had almost caught a moose, how he wrestled with it, but it got away. Fox said that he would go kill it.

"You are too small to kill it," laughed that Wolverine.

But after they parted, Fox went to where the moose was and he killed it. He skinned it and took some of the meat home to his family, who were all very hungry by now. After they had eaten he moved his whole family, including his married daughter, to a camp near the moose.

Wolverine was out hunting by himself, so he did know what had happened. At the moose camp they had enough meat for a long time.

When Wolverine finally found them at the camp, he was invited to eat, too. He ate and ate and ate until he was very full. He was so full that he grew tired and soon fell asleep. While he was asleep, Fox cooked a lot of fat. Then he carefully crept over to that place where *Naltsiis* was sleeping and he poured the burning hot grease all over Wolverine and killed him. He did this because Wolverine had been so selfish and greedy.

*Yanida'a* (yan-i-da-a) "mythic times/story time"
*Ciił Hwyaa* (keeth koo-yah) "Fox in *yanida'a*; smart man"
*Naltsiis* (nath-chees) "Wolverine"
*Deniigi* (den-nig-gee) "Moose" [bulls only]

Ahtna were found living in a variety of house types: dugouts, plank houses, or moose skin tent houses. This photo shows an Ahtna bark house. Photo circa 1906.

# Tazlina Lake Monster

*When I was a young boy—* Ciił Ggaay— *my grandmother told me this story about a monster that lived in Tazlina Lake, which is formed from the meltwater of Tazlina Glacier. Grandmother was born and raised at Tazlina Lake, which was abandoned around 1930 after disease killed many of the villagers there.*

Way long ago, back before there were white people in Ahtna country, there was a village at Tazlina Lake near Mendeltna Creek. When I was a little girl we lived there and we hunted sheep— *debae*— up in the mountains near the glacier. We had to walk there on a trail that went by the river for maybe forty miles.

A long time ago hunters used to hunt caribou—*udzih*— and catch salmon at Tazlina Lake. There was lots of caribou around. There still is sometimes. There were big moose sometimes, too.

Once in a while I heard stories about a giant monster that lived in the lake. People said they saw it sometimes. The stories say that it was so big that it could catch and eat whole caribou swimming across parts of the lake. It would come up from underneath and pull them under where it would eat them.

Because of their fear of the *gguux*— monster— Ahtna men avoided the middle of the lake which was very deep and rough.

*Ciił Ggaay* (keeth guy) "little boy"; *debae* (deb-a) "dall sheep"; *udzih* (you-jee) "caribou"; *gguux* (goo) "monster, or worm"

45

# Fox and Wolf

*This story, like* Fox and Wolverine, *also appeared in* Atna' Yanida'a *as told by* John Billum. *This version, told to me in my youth, is slightly different from that account.*

Once, way back in story time, when animals spoke and there were no people in Copper River country, there was this fox who acted just like people. He was very smart and a good hunter.

One day while he was out hunting, Fox came upon a track which he followed for a while. Soon he came upon a snare which someone had set to catch small animals. He kept following the tracks until he came upon an old woman Wolf—*Tikaani*— walking ahead of him.

Fox walked up to the old lady and spoke to her.

"Hello. I have not seen you before. Where are you from?"

The old woman replied, "Oh, I am from around here. What is your name?"

"I am *Ciił Hwyaa*," answered Fox.

The old lady *Tikaani* smiled as she spoke to him.

"Oh, you are a smart man." That is what she said.

"Yes," said Fox. "That is what my name means."

They spoke for a little while and then Fox left her. As he was walking along the trail ahead of her he came across another snare. He thought about a funny trick. He took off his clothes and stuffed them full of dried grass and moss so that it looked like him. Then he placed a large piece of fat—*tlagh*—on the breast. After he had done these things he placed it in the snare so that it looked as though he had been caught by the snare. Then he hid behind a tree and waited for the old woman to come along.

After a while the old lady came down the trail. She saw that her snare had caught that smart man and she ran up to it, smiling because she was so happy.

"You thought you were so smart. But I have caught you in my snare!" she said as she took out her skinning knife.

She took her knife and cut out the breast.

"Oh," she said. "Look how really fat it is." She was happy because meat with lots of fat is a good thing indeed. She cut some sticks nearby to roast the meat over a fire.

"This stick will be for my big brother, and this one is for my little brother." That is what she said while cutting them.

Now that she had her roasting sticks and a cooking fire, she took her knife and began to skin Fox. It didn't take long for her to learn that she had been tricked by that Fox.

"Oh! He is too smart for his own good," she said.

Hearing this, *Ciił Hwyaa* jumped out of his hiding place and laughed and laughed. He had really tricked her.

"Ha! Ha! You really thought you had me," laughed Fox.

The old lady wolf became angry and ran after him. They ran through the mountains where there was snow on the ground. The younger and faster Fox was too fast for the old lady and soon she became tired. When night came she froze to death. Then fox skinned her and took the meat back to the place where her snares were and he cooked the meat on her own roasting sticks.

Soon he heard sounds. Someone was coming. Fox hid behind a tree and waited. Then a whole family of wolves entered camp. They looked around and saw the meat cooking and saw that there was no one home. They thought this was their sister's camp, so they started to eat.

"This meat tastes like our sister," complained one of the wolves.

Just then Fox jumped out from his hiding place and began to laugh at the famly of wolves.

"Ha! Ha! Ha! You ate your sister!"

The angry wolves ran after that Fox. They chased him back up to the mountains. Fox tried to roll a big rock down on them but he couldn't move it. Instead, he hid behind it with a heavy club and waited. When one of the brothers walked by he killed him with the stick. Then he killed another.

After a while he had killed all but two of the wolves, who were too smart to go where their brothers had gone. They had become wise to Fox's tricks.

*Tikaani*  (tik-ah-nee)  "wolf"
*Ciił Hwyaa*  (keeth koo-yah)  "smart man; nick-name for Fox"
*tlagh* (tlah)  "fat, grease"

# Stone Woman

*Along the* Glenn Highway, *about half way between Anchorage and Glennallen, just a few miles northeast of the* Matanuska Glacier, *there is a giant rock— a mountain really— that rises steeply from the valley and is unlike the mountains around it. Ahtna Indians call it "Stone Woman Mountain" (its Ahtna name is* Natsede'aayi) *and there is a story about its origin. My uncle,* Herbert Smelcer, *told me this story years ago and* Harry Johns *of* Copper Center *later retold it to me.*

My father's family's clan is Talcheena Clan (while I am of the Indian Paint Clan— *tsisyu*— because of our matrilineal system). In our language, Talcheena means "came from the sea." It is said that long ago, before things became the way they are now, that Ahtna came from another place to settle this Copper River basin. This is the story of one woman back when people first moved from the sea to this country.

It is said that some people decided to move from the sea into Indian country, but to get there they would have to walk a long ways. They would have to cross many mountains, rivers, and glaciers. It would be very hard, especially for the very young and the very old.

To help them on their journey, Raven made the people become giants. They were much bigger than they are now. A hungry man could eat a whole caribou — *udzih* — at one sitting.

51

Raven's help made it easier for them people to climb the rugged mountains and cross the swift waters and dangerous glaciers. He helped the people, but he made them promise that they would not look back to where they came from; they could think only of where they were going.

"If someone looks back, something terrible will happen." That is what he said.

*Storyteller Harry Johns at Tazlina*

The people began their long march and just before they crossed into the country where Ahtna people now live, one of the young woman, who was carrying her baby— *sc'enggaay* – on her back, began to think about her home. She thought of what she was leaving behind. Maybe she liked her old home and didn't want to leave it. She became so homesick that she turned to look back in the direction from where she had come even though she had been told not to look back that way.

No sooner did she turn and look than she turned into stone. Because she was a giant, she became a giant rock. She turned into a mountain!

That young mother became a mountain because she did not listen to what that Raven had said to her and all those other Indians who were on that journey from the sea.

Today, people can still see her standing alone in the valley with that glacier and them mountains behind her.

And if you look close enough and you can still see her baby asleep on her back.

*tsisyu* (shi-shu) "Indian Paint Clan"
*udzih* (you-jee) "caribou" [as in *udzisyu*: Caribou Clan]
*sc'enggaay* (sken-guy) "baby; infant"

53

# Bush Indians

*Parents in many world cultures often warn their children that some boogeyman, gnome, fairy, or troll might take them away if they stray too far in the forest or go near forbidden places. They are invented to keep children from going near rivers, lakes, cliffs, or any place which may be dangerous to children. We have such creatures in our culture —we call them Bush Indians. Lucille Brenwick, born in Copper Center, related this account to me.*

When we were growing up back in the old days, our parents used to tell us that if we wandered too far away from camp, or went too near the river, that Bush Indians would get us.

Them Bush Indians werent' just your normal Indians. They say that they were taller than a big man, and they were hairy all over. I guess they must have looked kind of like Bigfoot. Them Bush Indians lived like savages in the woods and they captured little children as slaves. They say that they would even eat them

sometimes too. Whenever our parents didn't want us to go near some place they would tell us to watch out for Bush Indians. We'd be so scared, especially at night, that we'd just stay right close to our family. We wouldn't go anywhere.

They say that long time ago, a Bush Indian was wounded by Ahtna Indians. They say that he was hurt so bad that he later died after he got back to his people. He was buried up on the mountain, on *Kełt'aeni* — Mt. Wrangell — and that is why there is smoke coming from up there. It's his funeral flame burning.

*Kełt'aeni* (Kooth-taw-nee) "Mt. Wrangell"

# How Camprobber Got His Face

*This story is very much like the* Raven and Loon *story in that it tells how certain animals came to be the way they are (one of the primary purposes of myths). This narrative, though, involves* Woodpecker *and* Camprobber *(common gray jay). This particular retelling was told to me by my uncle,* Herbert Smelcer, *who was unable to recall where he first heard it.*

Back in *yanida'a,* when animals spoke and acted just like people, Camprobber— *stakalbaey—* and Woodpecker were friends. At least, they were friends until this one day.

Back in those times, those long ago times, Camprobber was completely gray and Woodpecker had long tail feathers— *t'aa.* That is the way it was back then.

One day, though, Camprobber and Woodpecker were talking to each other. They were standing near a campfire and speaking about something. Then they began to argue about something. Soon, Woodpecker became so mad that he grabbed Camprobber and shoved his face into the fire. He had ash all over his face!

*Stakalbaey* was very mad now, and as Woodpecker tried to fly away, he jumped up and grabbed his tailfeathers. He held on until all of the feathers were pulled right out of that Woodpecker's tail!

57

Since that time, Woodpeckers have no long tailfeathers, and camprobbers have spots on their face from the ash of the fire that Woodpecker pushed him into so long ago.

*yanida'a* (yan-i-da-a) "story time, mythic time"
*stakalbaey* (stok-all-bay) "camprobber (gray jay)"
*t'aa* (k-taw) "feathers" [pronounced as two syllables]

*My uncle, Herbert Smelcer, tells stories*

# *How Rabbit Got His Tail*

*This story is unique to Ahtna storytelling tradition. It is one of those wonderful stories that tells us how things came to be; in this case how rabbits got their small tails. While most myths are not place specific, that is they do not mention a specific location geographically, this one, like* "When They Killed the Monkey People" *does. A similar telling appears in* Atna' Yanida'a *and in* Indian Stories. *The latter, a narrative from* Cantwell, *was retold by* Jake Tansy.

A long time ago, an Indian from Tazlina Village went hunting along the Tazlina River near where it joins the Copper River. He hunted all day long until it became dark. Then he made a bed of spruce boughs to sleep upon. The sound of nearby running water soon put him to sleep.

After the man was gone for several days, some of the other men went out to search for him. They followed the trail along the Tazlina River until they came to its confluence with the Copper. There they found the dead hunter. They didn't know why he was dead—only that he had a small, round hole in his neck.

After a while, the people in the village began to forget about the dead hunter, and another man went hunting alone in the same place. When he didn't return, the people searched for him and found him dead in the same way as the first man.

Because the two men had died so strangely, the villagers became scared. They did not know what had happened to the two hunters, but they knew they didn't want the same thing to happen to them! They were so frightened that they stopped hunting and they stayed very close to the village. Soon, though, their food supplies ran low. They even ran out of dried salmon. The people became hungry.

The problem became worse and worse until one smart man, *Ciił Hwyaa*, decided to find out what was happening. He left one early morning and followed the same trail as the two hunters. He followed that trail down the Tazlina to where it ran into the Copper River. When he came to the place they had died, *Ciił Hwyaa* built a small camp.

On the way he had seen nothing strange— nothing to explain the men's deaths. But as he walked, he gathered large flat stones from along the river's edge. Since the hunters had small holes in their necks, he placed one flat stone against his neck and wrapped it with leather so that it could not be seen. He placed another stone under his clothes against his heart just in case. Once he had done these things, he pretended to go to sleep. He closed his eyes, but he was really awake. He was waiting for something to happen.

Soon, that smart man heard something in the woods. Something was coming down the trail and making a thumping sound. *Ciił Hwyaa* opened his eyes just a little and saw that it was only a rabbit— *ggax*— coming down the trail. The man lay quietly and waited for the rabbit. When it was close enough, the rabbit jumped into the air and landed on the man's neck with his sharp tail pointed downward.

You see, in the old times rabbits had sharply pointed tails which they used to protect themselves from other animals. But this mischievous rabbit had been using his tail to kill Indians while they were asleep.

When the rabbit came down on *Ciił Hwyaa's* neck, his sharp tail landed right on the flat stone. *Ggax* jumped high into the air and started screaming in pain. His tail was now all bent.

The hunter returned to his village and told the people what had happened. No one was ever killed by rabbits again, and since that time all rabbits have soft bent tails.

*Ciił Hwyaa* (keeth koo-yah) "smart man; sometimes used for Fox"
*ggax* (gok) "rabbit" [as in the name for "Gakona": *Ggax Kuna'*]

# Raven and Goose-Wife

*Every fall many Alaskan birds, especially waterfowl and arctic terns, migrate south to warmer climates. One word for fall translated means, "That time when birds gather to go to that place." But Ravens don't migrate. Raven stays near his people. This story, retold to me by my grandmother* Mary Smelcer-Wood, *also appears in* Han *and* Tanana *mythology.*

It is said that Raven once fell in love with a beautiful young goose woman. They stayed together all summer until summer came to its end. Snow began to fall in the mountains and nights became colder. It was time to fly south— time for birds to gather to go to that place.

The goose girl loved Raven, but she wanted to fly south with her relatives. Raven decided to go with her because he loved her so much and because she would not stay with him in *Atna' Nen'*—Indian Country.

Now, Raven can fly as well as any bird, but he cannot fly for very long at one time. He cannot fly very far without rest. In this way he is like *kuggaedi*, the mosquito. He tried to keep up with his wife and her relatives, but he was always tired and falling far behind. When the geese— *xax*— did stop to rest and eat, they stopped at places where there was no food for Raven. Because of this, he was growing weaker and weaker every day.

The geese were in a hurry to get away from the snow and cold, and they did not like waiting for that slow Raven. His goose-wife let him ride on her back, but she couldn't carry him that way for long. The goose-girl's parents and brothers each took turns carrying Raven on their backs, too. They took turns like that until they came to the ocean.

The father-in-law told Raven that the ocean was very wide and that it was very hard to cross. He told him how there would be no place for him to rest. Goose-Wife's father and brothers said that they would no longer carry Raven on their backs.

Raven thought about this and decided that he would have to stay. He said good-bye to his beloved wife and then he flew back into the country where he has lived ever since. Now ravens are here all the time because they can't fly south across the ocean like geese.


*Atna' Nen'* (Aht-na Nen) "Ahtna land, or Indian Country"
*kuggaedi* (koo-gad-ee) "mosquito"
*Xax* (kak) "goose; likely an onomatopoeia of a goose's sound"

# Spider Woman Story

*I have heard similar accounts of this narrative in the myth-
ologies of other Alaska Native Peoples. Indeed, there are numerous
stories involving* Spider Woman *in the mythologies of many
American Indian tribes as well. This particular version was told to me
at* Culture Camp *by* Ceclia Larson, *and later by her daughter, my
cousin,* Susan Larson. *Although scarey, it teaches an important
lesson to children.*

There were these two Indian girls. One was smarter than the
other. One day they were walking and they came to water— a
waterfall. They started sliding down the hill and they forgot to go
home. When they finally went home there was nobody there.
There was nobody at their house. Them girls looked all around
camp, but there was no sight of their family.

Pretty soon, them girls asked some seagulls— *nalbaey*— if
they knew where their mom and dad had gone. The birds said
that they didn't know.

Then that Camprobber— *stakalbaey*— came around and they
asked if he knew where their parents were.

"Can you tell us where our mom and dad have gone?" they
asked. "We'll give you a necklace if you tell us," they said.

*Stakalbaey* took the necklace. That's why his neck is white,
that camprobber. Then he told them what to do.

"Don't go on the wide road. Go on the narrow road." That's what he said to them.

After the bird flew away, the older sister started arguing with the younger sister saying, "We're supposed to go on the wide road. He said take the wide road." But the younger sister insisted that Camprobber had said to go on the narrow road. They argued like that for some time. Finally, though, that little girl gave up and went on the wide road because her older sister told her to.

A little ways down the wide road they came to a bad man. This old man— *da'atnac* — and his old wife were sitting in their cabin. He had a big pot cooking on the fire outside. Inside the pot he had dog eyes, bird eyes; all kinds of eyes boiling! The little girl became scared. Then the old man took an iron and put it in the fire until it was really hot. Then he used it to kill

*Susan Larson of Copper Center*

the big girl. But when he was about to do the same thing to the younger sister, the smart little girl spoke to the old man.

"I want to go to the bathroom," she said.

The old man told her, "No."

"I want to go to the bathroom. You can tie me around the waist with a rope and then let me go to the bathroom in the woods." That is what that smart young girl said to him.

The old woman gave her a comb for her hair. The girl put it into her pocket. Then she gave her other things too. The girl put them all into her pocket as well. Then the old woman told her to tie the rope to a stump. The young sister thanked her and then went out alone to go to the bathroom.

When she was far enough in the woods that the old man could no longer see her, the young girl untied herself and put the rope around a tree stump. Then she started running. She ran as fast as she could.

After enough time had passed the old man yelled for the girl to return. When she did not answer he started to pull on the rope. He could feel her weight on it, but when he brought the rope all the way to camp he saw that it was only a stump. Oh, he was mad! He started running after that girl and yelling at her.

The frightened girl was running so fast that she dropped the comb and it turned into brush. She dropped many things while she was running, and whatever she dropped turned into things like hills and mountains and things. This slowed the man down.

Finally, she came upon a spider's house. It was Spider Woman's house. The young sister asked her for help.

"Can you tell me where my mom and dad have gone? I'm running from that old man who killed my sister," she said.

Spider Woman wrapped her up in a cacoon and hid her under her bed. When the old man came to the house he started knocking on the doors and windows. Spider Woman killed him somehow. When it was safe she started asking the girl questions.

"Do you want to see your family? You can see them," she said.

The smart young girl told her that she did want to see her parents again.

"See that big long rope? You need to fix it." That's what Spider Woman said to her.

The girl saw the rope made of spider's silk and agreed to fix it. Later, the woman told her to move a rock, but it was too big and she couldn't move it. That woman hit the rock with a stick and it went away. The girl looked at the hole where the rock had been and she could see her mom and dad all walking around.   The girl began to cry. She wanted to go home.

Then Spider Woman took the thin, long rope that had been repaired and threw it down the hole after tying off one end.

"Do you want to go home now?" she asked.

The smart girl said that she did want to go home.

"Then I'm going to put you down on that string and you must close your eyes. If you open your eyes before the end you'll come back  up here." That's what Spider Woman said.

*Cecilia Larson at Culture Camp*

Before the girl reached the bottom of the rope she opened her eyes because she couldn't wait to see her family. But as soon as she did, she was right back at the top again and had to do it all over again. Finally, though, she climbed all the way down and her parents saw her. They were sad that her older sister was gone, but they were happy that their young, smart daughter was with them again.

*nalbaey*  (nall-bay)  "sea gull"
*stakalbaey*  (stok-all-bay)  "camprobber; gray jay"
*da'atnae*  (da-ot-na)  "old man; not very old man, though"

# Old Man and Grizzly

*This tale of respect may be more oral history than it is mythology. I have heard a similar account told by* Tanacross Indians *in the area near* Tok, *which is just outside of Ahtna Country. Although a narrative in both tribes, it may have actually been an Ahtna story first. Indeed, through intermarriage, many Indians in that area are of Ahtna descent.*

Way up in northeastern Ahtna country, there is a story of a very Old Man—*nest'e'*—who lived in a small village where there is no village today. It may have been only a summer camp. It was midsummer and there were salmon everywhere. In all of the streams and rivers there were plenty of salmon—*łuk'ae*.

Some young boys wanted to go down by the river. This very Old Man asked if he could go with them. He was so old that he was bent over and used a stick when he walked. The boys didn't want the useless old man to go with them, but he did anyhow, and he was able to keep up with them.

They were walking down by the river when they saw a big grizzly— *Tsaani*. Those boys started teasing the bear. They threw rocks and sticks at it and called it names.

"*Tsaani*, you are afraid of boys!" they laughed.

They had no respect for the bear. The very Old Man told them to stop, but them boys just kept on teasing that bear. They wouldn't listen to that man because he was so old.

Finally, the grizzly stopped and looked at them. Then it started walking towards them. When it came close the boys became afraid and ran away, leaving the old man to face the angry bear alone.

When it was very close, that bear charged the Old Man. The young boys thought surely the old man would be killed. But, when the bear was almost upon him, the man stood as tall as he could and held his arms far apart with the walking stick in one hand. Then he yelled at the bear.

That bear didn't know what to think. He just stopped and sat down—his small dark eyes looking at the old man.

The very Old Man wasted no time. He hit the bear across the nose with his stick. That bear howled in pain and ran away. The old man had scared the bear away with only a walking stick!

Them boys who had watched the whole thing from far away learned something that day. From then on they showed respect for elders and they never teased bears again.

*nest'e'* (nest-a) "very old man; not just an older man"
*łuk'ae* (thlook-a) "salmon [in general]"
*tsaani* (chaw-nee) "grizzly bear"

# *Owl Story*

*Just as parents told children about* Bush Indians *to keep them close to home and out of trouble, so too would they tell stories of* Owl *to keep small children from crying, especially at night. This narrative was told by* Markle Pete *of* Tazlina Village.

When I was a little boy, my parents told me stories about Owl— *Besiini.* They told us that we should never cry at night, especially if we were at camp. They said that *Besiini* hears crying children because he has such good hearing. Owl didn't like to hear crying children. That's what they told us Indian kids way back when I was growing up.

They said that if a crying child was in the woods, Owl would swoop down and cut off their feet. He would cut them off just below the ankles. He did this only to them children who were crying. Some of the stories were really scarey. We were afraid to hear them sometimes.

One story said that a very young child, a baby really, was inside a house at night and crying. It cried and cried. That night *Besiini* flew in through an open window and took the baby away and ate it! Owl either cuts off children's feet or kills them for crying too much!

I remember one night when I was a young boy. I had heard the stories that day. I thought about them stories all day long. I couldn't stop thinking about *Besiini* chasing after children to cut off their feet.

That night, when I was already in bed, I heard Owl outside my window.

"Whoo. Whoo." He must have been pretty close by.

I was so scared I jumped into bed with my mom and dad. My dad yelled at me, "What are you doing in our bed?"

I just crawled further under them blankets and said to my dad, "Hold on to my feet dad! Hold on to my feet!"

My parents just laughed and laughed.

*Markle Pete of Tazlina tells stories*

*Tazlina* (Taz-lee-naw) "village and river name; [swift water]"
*Besiini* (bess-ee-nee) "Owl"

72

# The Man With Too Many Wives

*In my book,* The Raven and the Totem, *I retold a similar story from* Yupik *(Central Eskimo) in which the wife turns into a bear to seek revenge by killing the unfaithful husband. In another Ahtna variation, the young woman is actually a mouse—*dluuni.

Long, long time ago, there was a man who had two wives. He would go hunting for days looking for food. He would be gone for many days at a time.

One day, while he was hunting far from home, the man came upon a small house. It was the house of a beautiful, young single woman. He did not tell her that he had two wives. Because the woman thought that he was single too, she agreed to live with him in her house.

The man, who now had three wives in two different houses, would hunt for both households. He would bring only the best meat—*c'etsen'*—to his new wife, and he brought only poor meat to his other two wives. It went on like that for a while—him living in one house for a few days and then in the other for a few days. Each time he would leave, the wives thought that he was only going hunting.

After a time, though, the two wives became suspicious.

"Why does our husband only bring us such poor meat?" they wondered.

One day the man returned with really poor moose meat. The women asked about the rest of the moose, but the husband said that this is all that he got from the moose.

73

Next time that man left, one of them wives followed him. She followed him for most of a day until they came upon a house. As he approached, a beautiful, younger woman came out of the house and greeted the man. They both went inside and he did not come out for a long time.

As soon as he was gone, the first wife went up to the house. She introduced herself but did not mention that she was married to the same man.

"Where do you come from?" asked the young woman.

"I live far away. That is why you haven't seen me before," replied the older woman.

The younger, new wife was making oil from meat. She was boiling fat in a pot while they spoke.

The young wife started talking about how wonderful her new husband was— how he always brought her the best meat. The older woman became angry. Soon, she shoved the younger woman's head into the boiling pot of oil and killed her. Then she propped up her head with a stick so that it looked as if she was still stirring the boiling pot. Then she hid and waited.

When the husband came home he saw his new wife. It looked like she was stirring the cooking pot. He went over to hold her, but as he did she fell over. She was dead. The man cried and cried.

"My wife! My wife!" he kept saying.

The first wife who was hiding ran back to their house and told the other wife what had happened. When the man came home they did not let him know that they knew what had happened. But from then on he brought home only the best meat and the two women were happy.


*dluuni* (dloo-nee) "mouse"
*c'etsen'* (ket-chen) "meat"

# The House of Wind

*This particular story teaches how to behave properly in society. I have heard several different versions (as most stories have depending on who told them and where), but this one is adapted from* Atna' Yanida'a *as told by* John Billum *of* Chitina.

Once, long ago, Fox's daughter was married to Raven. They lived with her parents because they did not have a house of their own yet.

One day, while hunting far from home, Fox came upon a small house in the woods. He had never seen it before. There was no one around so he went inside. Everything was very neat and clean. There was lots of food, too.

"This is a very nice house," thought Fox.

He looked around but he touched nothing, and then he sat down to rest.

Soon a voice said, "What a good man he is. So honest. Surely he must be hungry. Let's give him something to eat."

That is what the voice said even though Fox didn't see anyone around that house. You see, it was the house of the Wind. Soon, food came flying to Fox. He ate things such as fish, meat, and berries—*gigi*. Everything tasted very good.

When it was time to leave, the voice spoke again.

"Let's give him something to take home."

Again, like before, things came flying to Fox. This time it was moose hides, necklaces, and moccasins— *kentsiis*. More meat also came to him. He put these things into his pack until it was very full. Before he left he thanked the voices and told them how much he liked their house—*hnax*. The pack was so heavy that Fox could barely carry it. When he returned home, Raven, his new son-in-law, saw the filled pack. He asked Fox where he got these things and Fox told him the story.

"Why didn't you just take everything since there was no one in the house?" asked Raven.

Fox replied, "It is not the right thing to do. You must sit still and touch nothing in someone else's home." That is what he said.

"If I had been there, " said that Raven, "I would have taken everything."

The next day Raven said he was going to find the house. Fox told him to sit still and quiet and to touch nothing inside.

When Raven found the house, he went inside and asked aloud if there was anyone home. When no one answered he walked all over the house and ate the food that was there and filled his pack with everything that he could.

Soon, he heard a voice.

"What a bad person you are. You just take whatever is not yours."

Raven went to where the sound came from and threw things at it. Then he quickly left the strange house. But before he was home, the wind picked up and a stick flew at him and hit his head, knocking him down hard. Then the pack was lifted by the wind and carried back to Wind's House.

Raven told Fox what had happened. Fox was not surprised. "You see," he said. "I told you not to touch anything and to sit still. It is wrong to take things like that."


*gigi* (kih-kih) "berry" [G̲ pronounced as a cross between G̲ and K̲]
*kentsiis* (ken-chees) "moccasins"
*hnax* (nock) "house"

# How Raven Made Salmon Swim

*Although quite brief, this story illustrates how Raven made things the way they are. I have heard this story from my grandmother,* Mary Smelcer-Wood, *and again at* Culture Camp *by* Fred Ewan *who told it to a group of Indian children while teaching salmon cutting at the fishwheel.*

Way long ago, before there were people, Raven had already created everything, including salmon. He had made the rivers and mountains, and the animals and birds. He created salmon to join the streams and rivers with the sea.

But even though Raven made salmon, they couldn't swim well because they weren't heavy enough. You see, they had a pocket of air inside their head. Because of this they would always float to the surface where they were too easy prey for Grizzly Bear—*Tsaani*—and Eagle—*sgulak*.

One day when Raven was flying around, he noticed how much trouble salmon were having swimming and he decided to help them. He flew down to the chief of the Salmon People and spoke to him.

"Why is it that you seem to have so much trouble swimming?" he asked the fish.

The Chief of the Salmon People replied, "Our heads have air inside which makes us float. It is very hard to swim under water when our head keeps floating to the surface."

Raven thought about how to fix them. Then he lifted the chief of the Salmon People from the water and carefully placed a

small stone inside his head. When *Saghani Ggaay*—Trickster Raven replaced the fish into the Copper River, it sank near the bottom and didn't float back to the surface.

*Fred Ewan teaches fish cutting at Culture Camp*

"*Tsin'aen,*" said the salmon to Raven, thanking him for what he had done.

From that time on, all salmon swim near the bottom of the rivers where they are not such easy meals for other animals. When we cut them up for drying and smoking, we can still see the tiny rocks in their head which Raven put there long ago.

*tsaani* (chaw-nee) "grizzly Bear"
*sgulak* (sgoo-lack) "eagle" [loanword?]
*Saghani Ggaay* (sa-gaw-nee guy) "Raven; in storytime"
*tsin'aen* (chin-nen) "thank you"

# When They Killed the Monkey People

*The story of the* Cet'aeni— *"The Tailed Ones" or "Monkey People"— is very regional. It is unique to Upper Ahtna oral history and does not appear in the stories of neighboring Indian tribes. This version, which differs from some accounts, was retold by* Markle Pete *and my grandmother,* Mary Smelcer-Wood. *Another retelling can be found in* Tatl'ahwt'aenn Nenn', *as told by* Fred John *of* Mentasta.

This story comes from upriver, mostly in the Mentasta area, but most Ahtna people have heard this story at one time or another. I heard it even when I was a young child.

A long time ago, but not back in *yanida'a*, maybe in the past couple hundred years, there were these long-tailed creatures living up around Batzulneta or around Slana. Somewhere up there. We called them *Cet'aeni*, or the "Monkey People."

These tailed-ones were kind of human-like. They walked on their hind legs, but they were hairy all over. They did not wear any clothes, and they had long tails.

It began that people started to disappear from this country. All kinds of people would disappear— children, old people, even young men and women, too. Them Monkey People were killing them. It got so bad that Indians were afraid to go out alone. They were killing so many Ahtna that they might kill them all if they weren't stopped.

So, this one young man, who was brave and smart, he decided to find the *Cet'aeni*. He was very smart. One day after a man came running back to camp saying that he had seen a Tailed One near a treefall, the young man went there by himself.

He did not want the *Cet'aeni* to know that he was around, so he covered his footprints with grass. That way they could not see his tracks.

After a while, he came upon several Monkey People. There was a tree nearby so he climbed it. He climbed way up to the top so that the wind would carry his scent away. This way the *Cet'aeni* would not know that he was watching them.

Safe in his tree— *ts'abaeli*— the young man watched as the Monkey People played some game with what looked like a ball. But when he looked closer, he saw that it was really a human skull! They were throwing a human skull around like a ball! It was the skull of a young Indian man who had disappeared not long ago.

Just then it began to rain. The Tailed Ones didn't like the rain and so they started down the trail. The smart young man followed them, but he stayed far enough behind so that they did not know he was there.

After a while they came to a cliff by the river. Near the top of the cliff were eight caves, just big enough for a man to fit through. The *Cet'aeni* went up the side of the cliff and into the caves. That is where they lived.

The young man ran back to the village and told his people that he knew where they lived. The people gathered their spears and bows and arrows and left for the cliff with the cave in it. The women gathered dry branches and green branches along the way.

When they finally came to the caves, they saw many bones scattered all around the entrances. They were human bones! The women placed the dry branches in the entrances and lit a fire. As the fire grew hot, they threw green branches onto the fire. This made it begin to smoke. The dark smoke, made from the green boughs, filled the caves quickly.

Soon, the Monkey People began to come out of their houses. The smoke made it so that they could not see or breathe well. When they came out of the caves the Indian men killed them with spears and arrows and clubs. They killed all of them and only one Indian was killed in the battle. After that day, no more Ahtna people were killed by *Cet'aeni*. If they hadn't killed them, they surely would have killed all of the Ahtna and then there wouldn't be Indians in Copper River country—*Atna' Nen'*—today.

People who have been in that area say that you can still see the cave up on the cliff just above the river. They say you can see the charcoal remains there, too.

*yanida'a* (yan-i-da-a) "story time, mythic times"
*Cet'aeni* (Ket-tan-ee) "Monkey People, or Tailed Ones"
*ts'abaeli* (cha-bal-ee) "tree"
*Atna' Nen'* (aht-naw nen) "Copper River country"

# The Boy Who Offended Salmon

*In most cultures, the animals which provide food and clothing, although hunted or trapped, must be treated with respect. There are numerous Alaska Native myths which tell of these taboos, or in Ahtna, 'engii. Indeed, traditionally, adolescent children and menstruants were not allowed to handle salmon, and fresh-caught fish could not be eaten until one day after its capture (big game meat, it was said, could not be eaten until three days after it had been killed). A version of this narrative was first recorded by* Fredrica de Laguna.

Once there was a young Indian boy who lived in a small village along the river. As with most Ahtna communities, most of the villagers were relatives and members of his clan.

During the summer, all of the adults were busy catching salmon—*łuk'ae*—which they would smoke and dry or boil to make fish oil. This is how things were back then. Everyone worked to put away food for winter. Without salmon, people would surely starve in winter. They used almost all of the fish. They even made fishhead soup from it.

It is important to show respect for the salmon. If we offend them by wasting their flesh, then they might not come again next year. If we did not return their bones to the river so that their spirits could rejoin their kin, then they might not return as well. Salmon are so important that June is called *Łuk'ae Na'aaye'*.

Although young children could not handle freshly-caught fish, and they could not cut it up for hanging on drying racks, they were oftentimes asked to throw the fish bones back into the river after the meat had been eaten. This one boy was lazy and dis-

87

respectful. One day he was told to throw a bunch of fish bones back into the river. But because it was further than he cared to walk, that boy just went in the woods behind his house and threw them bones onto the dirt. He kicked some more dirt upon them to cover up what he had done. Later that night, when he was given a piece of dried salmon, he complained that he was tired of fish and he threw it into the fire when no one was looking.

Soon the salmon run became very small. Fewer and fewer fish were caught in nets each day. The people began to worry that there would not be enough salmon put away for winter.

Each day, when asked to return the fish bones to the river, that boy would throw them on the ground instead. Sometimes he would just cover them up with a few branches or twigs. Each time he did this, fewer salmon were caught the next day.

One day, the boy was walking a little ways from fish camp when he heard something talking from the river. It was a voice calling to him. He walked over to where it came, but he saw nothing. Then the voice came from upriver a little ways. It came from below a steep bank at the river's edge. The boy laid upon his belly and hung over the edge to see who it was speaking to him from the water. Just then the bank gave way, and the boy fell into the dark, swift water.

It was the Salmon Chief —*Łuk'ae Kaskae* — who had tricked him. Now that boy was taken by the Salmon People for what he had done to their relatives.

*'engii* (en-gee) "taboo, that which is forbidden"
*Łuk'ae Na'aaye'* (Thlook-a Naw-eye) "Salmon Month"
*Łuk'ae Kaskae* (Thlook-a Kass-ka) [ a as in "cat"] "Salmon Chief"

Diane Crown, 1982

# When Raven Killed Porcupine

*This story was originally told by* Jake Tansy *of* Cantwell, *the northwestern-most Ahtna village located just outside of Denali National Park. Jake was born at* Valdez Creek *in 1906. A similar version of this story appeared in* Indian Stories *(1982), a small limited printing bilingual collection of Cantwell Indian stories.*

A long time ago, just like today, Indians hunted porcupine *nuuni*. But long ago, some people way up near Tyone Lake would go hunting for porcupines and never return. They just disappeared. The villagers became scared, so they planned a war against the porcupine who must be killing all of them hunters.

Raven heard their plans and decided to go find that porcupine himself. He flew down the Tyone River into upper Susitna country until he came to where the *nuuni* lived. Way up in a tree sat the very big porcupine eating bark. It was truly the biggest porcupine he had ever seen.

Raven hid behind some bushes and waited until he came down from the tree. When Porcupine finally came down, Raven walked over to him quietly. *Nuuni* heard something behind him and flared out his quills. He had many long, sharp quills— *c'ok* on his back.

Raven stopped and spoke to him.

"I come to tell you something important," he said.

"What news do you bring me?" asked Porcupine.

Raven told him that the villagers planned a war against him. He told him that they were even now gathering upriver preparing for war with many bows and arrows.

Porcupine was worried.

"What should I do?" he asked.

That tricky Raven had an idea.

"Are you skillful enough to catch their arrows as they shoot them at you?

"I don't know," said *Nuuni*.

Raven told the porcupine that he would train him. He started by shooting an arrow at him very slowly. It was so slow that Porcupine easily caught it. Then Raven shot the next arrow slightly faster. Each time *Nuuni* caught the arrow—*cenk'a'*—in the air and was unharmed. They trained like that all day until Raven was shooting arrows very fast and Porcupine was able to catch them without being hurt.

Then Raven shot at a stump just to the side of the big porcupine and struck it in the middle. The arrow was shot fast and it stuck deep into the stump.

*Nuuni* went over to take out the arrow. While he was trying to pull it from the stump, Raven aimed and shot Porcupine below the armpit near where his heart was, killing him. He died because he was shot in his *ciz'aani*, his heart.

Raven flew down to where the villagers gathered and told them what he had done. From then on, no villagers were killed when they went porcupine hunting.

*nuuni*  (new-nee)  "porcupine"

*c'ok*  (kee*awk)  "quills"  [*pronounced as one syllable]

*cenk'a'*  (kenk-a)  "arrow"  [a̲ pronounced as in 'cat']

*ciz'aani*  (kiz-aw-nee)  "heart"

# The Woman Taken By A Bear

*This story was also originally told by* Jake Tansy *of* Cantwell
*in* Indian Stories *(1982). His daughter,* Lousie Tansy Mayo,
*translated the narratives from western Ahtna dialect into English. In
many Athabaskan storytelling traditions, there are stories of bears
abducting and even marrying women.*

There was a potlatch a long time ago. It was a big potlatch
and everyone was invited. People were sent to tell neighboring
villages about it. Even Bear—*Tsaani*—was told about it.

In the village where the potlatch was held, there lived a
beautiful young woman. Bear saw her go inside the sweathouse
alone. While she was still inside, *Tsaani* reached in and pulled her
out by her long, black hair. Then he ran away from the village
with her. He took her up to a mountain ridge before he stopped.

"This is my home," he said. "Stay close to the fire and don't
run away." That is what he told her.

The woman didn't run away because she didn't even know
where she was. Bear went off to get some cooking sticks. After he
was out of sight, the girl looked around the camp. She saw a
mouse—*dluuni*—nearby and it spoke to her.

"That bear is really a bad person," it said. "You must get
away from him. I will help you."

*Dluuni* gave her a feather and a sewing needle which she

93

put in her hair. Then he gave her some meat.

A little later, *Tsaani* came back with roasting sticks— *gges*. He saw the meat and cooked some to eat. He had planned to eat the woman, but he ate the meat for now. When they had eaten, he said they would go down to a nearby lake. They went down the mountain to the lake which was frozen. It was barely frozen, though. You could see right through it. The ice was still thin.

"You walk out on the lake first and then I will," said Bear.

As the beautiful woman walked out towards the middle of the lake— *ben,* the ice began to sag and make cracking sounds. But because she was wearing the feather that mouse had given her, she did not break through. She had become light because of the feather— *t'aa.*

She walked back to the edge. Now it was *Tsaani's* turn. That big bear walked slowly and carefully, but when he was in the middle of the lake he fell through the ice. The water was deep and cold, and Bear could not get out. He was in trouble. He asked the girl to help him.

"If you help me, I will take you home," he said. That is what he promised her. He made a promise.

But after the girl helped him, Bear forgot all about what he had said and he did not take her home to her people.

The next day he took her down to the lake again. This time, when she was half way across, Bear stomped his foot and said, "Lake, be a lake again."

Suddenly the ice became even thinner and one of the girl's feet fell through. But only one. She carefully lifted her foot out of the water and walked back to shore because of her feather.

When it was Bear's turn, the young woman waited until he was in the middle and then she stomped her foot and said, "Be a lake again."

Suddenly, the ice became very thin and Bear fell through. Again he promised to take the girl home if she pulled him out.

"No, you promised me that yesterday and you didn't take me home," replied the woman who had been taken by the bear.

"This time I'm telling the truth," he said. "I promise to take you home."

The woman helped him out of the water. After Bear dried off, he lowered his back so that she could sit on him, and they started off with her on his back. But it wasn't really the trail to her village. Instead, it was the path to Bear's nephews' house. When he was close to their house, *Tsaani* told her to walk the rest of the way by herself. He knew that his nephews would eat her when she came upon them up the trail.

A little later, she came upon Bear's hungry nephews. They chased her, but before they caught her she turned into a feather! She became a feather. The bears jumped up to get her, but they could not catch her. Then, while she was a feather in the air, that woman turned into a long sewing needle and she pierced the bears in the heart, killing them. Then she turned back into a person again.

When she had walked down the trail a ways, she came upon *Tsaani*. He was very surpised that she was still alive. He thought that she must have somehow killed his nephews. This scared Bear who thought maybe she could kill him, too.

Finally, Bear agreed to take her home. He put her on his back and carried her across the country and over the mountain until she was home again.

*Tsaani* (chaw-nee) "grizzly bear"
*dluuni* (dloo-nee) "mouse"
*gges* (gess) "roasting stick"
*ben* (ben) "lake"
*t'aa* (k-taw) "feather" [pronounced as two syllables]

# Giant Killer

*Stories of Little People and of giants are found in the mythologies of many world cultures. These stories exist in the narratives of such distant and diverse cultures as Irish and Eskimo; in the European accounts of gnomes, trolls, and borrowers; and in the oral traditions of Ahtna. This story was narrated by* John Billum *in* Chitina.

In the far time, when things were not as they are today, there lived in Indian Country a giant man and a giant woman. While the man never harmed the little Ahtna People, the woman giant was always killing them, like ants— *nadosi—* beneath her feet.

One day a young Indian man was hunting. He found a porcupine den and he crawled inside to catch the *nuuni* that lived there. While he was inside a shadow fell across the entrance and blocked the sunlight. The young man wondered what it could be that blocked the sun. He looked out the hole and saw this giant man.

"Come out and talk to me," said the giant.

The Indian was scared. He had never before seen a giant, though he had heard stories about them and how Indians were killed by them.

"I am Nigi Giidzi," said the giant. "Come out from the den. I need your help. I will not harm you."

The young man crawled out from the den and stood in front of the giant, barely coming up to his knees.

"What can I do to help you?" asked the Indian.

The giant named Nigi Giidzi told him about the woman giant. He told him how she always killed the little Indians. He told him that he wanted to kill her, but that she was too strong and cunning to defeat on his own.

"While I am fighting with her, you will come out from a hiding place and cut the tendons of her heel. Then she will not be able to stand up and I will be able to get rid of her."

That is what the giant said to the little man.

The Indian agreed, and so Nigi Giidzi placed him upon his shoulder and they walked for a long time until they found the giant woman eating several mountain sheep.

The two giants fought, and the little man helped the giant get rid of the woman giant and all of the little people were saved.

*nadosi* (na-doe-see) "ant" [specifically: carpenter ant]
*nuuni* (new-nee) "porcupine"

# About the Authors

John E. Smelcer (Ahtna descendant) is the Executive Director of the Ahtna Heritage Foundation and faculty of Humanities at Embry-Riddle Aeronautical University. He is the author of several collections of Alaska Native myths and oral narratives, of encyclopedia articles on Alaska Native cultures, American Indian biographies and ANSCA, and of a collection of poems written in Ahtna with English translations. His recent volume of poetry, *Tracks*, includes an introduction by Carl Sagan. Several of his stories appear in *The Last New Land: Stories of Alaska, Past and Present*. In 1994, he edited *Durable Breath: Contemporary Native American Poetry*. His poetry appears in *Native American Songs and Poems* and in such magazines as *The Atlantic Monthly*. He has held visiting faculty posts at universities around the world. Poet, teacher, nature writer, anthropologist, and linguist, he is currently working with tribal elders to revise the *Ahtna Noun Dictionary*.

Gary Snyder, won the Pulitzer Prize in 1975 for his book *Turtle Island*. The author of sixteen books of poetry and prose, mostly recently of *Mountains and Rivers Without End*, he has been a Guggenheim Fellow and is a member of the American Academy of Arts and Letters and the American Academy of Arts and Sciences. He is a professor of English at the University of California at Davis.